THE GREAT DINOSAUR SEARCH

Rosie Heywood

Illustrated by Studio Galante and Inklink Firenze

Edited by Philippa Wingate
Managing designer: Mary Cartwright
Scientific consultant: Dr. David Norman

With thanks to John Russell, Natalie Abi-Ezzi,
Rebecca Mills and Katarina Dragoslavić

Contents

Archaeothyris had two large, spiky teeth which it used to kill its prey. Find three.

The first **snails** appeared on land at this time. Before, they had lived underwater. Spot ten.

Lizard-like **Microsaurs** lived on land but laid their eggs in water. Spot 11.

Ophiderpeton had no arms or legs, and looked like an eel. Can you spot five?

Spiders spun simple webs to catch their prey. Find seven.

Westlothiana was a reptile. It laid eggs with hard shells and lived on dry land. Spot ten.

Eogyrinus was the size of a crocodile. It snapped up fish in its powerful jaws. Find four.

Gerrothorax lay at the bottom of rivers, waiting to catch passing fish. Spot one.

Giant **millipedes** fed on rotting leaves. Spot five.

Rocky landscape

During this time, lots of animals appeared that could live on land. The most striking of these had huge sails on their backs. Many of these creatures died out before the arrival of the dinosaurs.

Yougina had strong, sharp teeth for cracking open snail shells. Spot three.

Pareiasaurus grew as big as a hippopotamus. Spot three.

Protorosaurus reared up on its back legs to catch insects to eat. Find four.

Sphenacodon had a ridge on its back. Spot six.

Seymouria couldn't move fast on land. It spent most of its time in water. Spot three.

Scientists know Sauroctonus was a meat-eater, because its teeth were long and sharp. Find four.

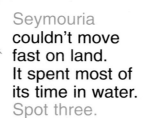

Diadectes had legs which stuck out on either side of its body, just like a modern lizard. Spot seven.

Edaphosaurus warmed itself up by letting the Sun heat the blood in a sail on its back. Spot 11.

Moschops was the size of a cow. Spot four.

Cacops had a huge head compared to the size of its body. Spot nine.

Long bones sticking out from Dimetrodon's spine held up a sail on its back. Find five.

Eryops was a distant relative of modern frogs. Spot two.

Anteosaurus bit chunks of flesh off its prey, then swallowed them whole. Spot two.

Casea had teeth all over the roof of its mouth, to crush up plants. Find four.

Scutosaurus had thick skin, and spikes sticking out of its cheeks. Spot three.

Bradysaurus had a neck frill at the back of its skull. Find one.

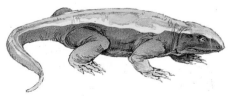

The first dinosaurs

About 225 million years ago, the first dinosaurs appeared. There are six different kinds of dinosaurs to spot here, along with some of the other strange creatures that lived at the same time.

Kuehneosaurus had thin sails of skin, which it used to glide from tree to tree. Spot four.

Although Cynognathus looked a little like a dog, it had scaly skin. Spot one.

Terrestrisuchus was about the size of a squirrel. Can you spot eight?

The dinosaur Staurikosaurus probably hunted in packs. Can you find seven?

The dinosaur Plateosaurus, could rear up on its back legs. Find six.

Rutiodon had nostrils on the top of its head, between its eyes. Find two.

Ticinosuchus had strong, long legs so it could move very quickly. Spot five.

Saltopus, a dinosaur, scampered over rocks searching for lizards to eat. Find ten.

Syntarsus had sharp eyes and great speed to help it catch its prey. Spot four.

Peteinosaurus was one of the first flying lizards. Find three.

Placerias lived in herds and roamed long distances in search of food. Spot ten.

Desmatosuchus had long spikes sticking out from its shoulders. Spot three.

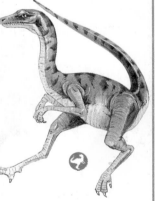

The dinosaur Coelophysis was a skilful hunter. Find seven.

Anchisaurus was one of the first dinosaurs. It was 2½m (8ft) long. Spot five.

Stagonolepis may have dug for roots with its snout. Can you spot four?

Thrinaxodon had whiskers on its face and a furry body. Find five.

In the forest

The largest dinosaurs ever to walk the Earth lived at this time. Growing to enormous sizes, these giant creatures fed on the lush trees and plants which grew in the warm, wet climate.

Brachiosaurus' nostrils were on the top of a bump on its head. Spot one.

Pterodactylus snapped insects out of the air as it flew. Spot ten.

Apatosaurus swallowed leaves whole, because it could not chew. Spot five.

Camptosaurus could run on its back legs if it was chased. Find two.

Fierce meat-eater **Ceratosaurus** had over 70 saw-edged fangs. Spot one.

Compsognathus is one of the smallest known dinosaurs. It was no bigger than a cat. Find eight.

Camarasaurus ate leaves from the lower tree branches. Spot three.

Diplodocus was as long as three buses parked end to end. Can you spot six?

Dryosaurus may have lived in herds like modern deer. Spot 17.

Archaeopteryx was probably the first bird. It flew from tree to tree. Find three.

Kentrosaurus had large spines on its back and tail. Spot one.

Scaphognathus had excellent eyesight. Can you find two?

Allosaurus had bony ridges above its eyes. Spot three.

Ornitholestes used its sharp claws to grab lizards and other small animals. Spot three.

Coelurus had long legs and could run fast to catch its prey. Spot two.

The bony plates on Stegosaurus' back may have absorbed heat from the Sun. Find two.

15

In the ocean

While dinosaurs roamed the land in Jurassic times, huge reptiles swam through the vast oceans.

There are 87 creatures to spot on these two pages. How many you can find?

Brittle stars still live in today's oceans. They have five long arms. Spot eight.

Plesiosaurus flapped its fins slowly up and down like a turtle. Find two.

Sharks sank to the bottom of the ocean if they didn't keep swimming. Spot six.

Pleurosaurus had a long body and an even longer tail. Can you spot four?

Liopleurodon ate other large sea creatures such as Ichthyosaurs. Spot one.

Pleurosternon needed to go up to the surface to breathe. Can you spot two?

Rhomaleosaurus was as big as a modern killer whale, and just as fierce. Spot two.

16

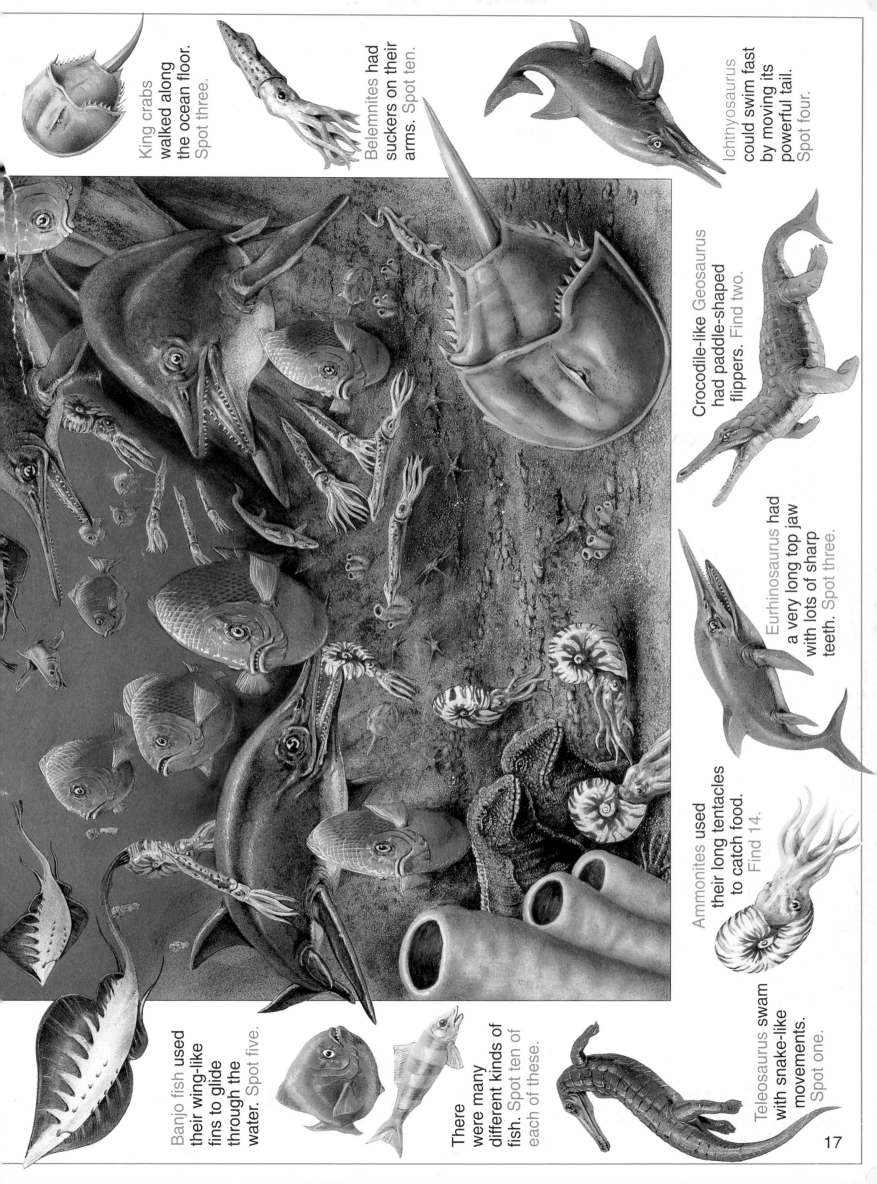

King crabs walked along the ocean floor. Spot three.

Belemnites had suckers on their arms. Spot ten.

Ichthyosaurus could swim fast by moving its powerful tail. Spot four.

Crocodile-like Geosaurus had paddle-shaped flippers. Find two.

Eurhinosaurus had a very long top jaw with lots of sharp teeth. Spot three.

Ammonites used their long tentacles to catch food. Find 14.

Banjo fish used their wing-like fins to glide through the water. Spot five.

There were many different kinds of fish. Spot ten of each of these.

Teleosaurus swam with snake-like movements. Spot one.

17

Dusty desert

The dinosaurs that lived in desert areas of what is now Mongolia and China suffered terrible dust storms. Some choked to death, while others were buried alive in sand dunes.

Oviraptor built nests for their eggs and sat on them until they hatched. Spot 12.

Psittacosaurus had a bony beak like a parrot's. Find four adults and six young.

Tarbosaurus ran after its prey with powerful bursts of speed. Can you find one?

Saurolophus had a bony spike on top of its head. Spot four.

These lizards fed on dinosaur eggs. Find eight.

If Pinacosaurus was attacked, it used the club on its tail as a weapon. Spot two.

Protoceratops laid
its eggs in nests
in the sand.
Find five.

Protoceratops' nest

Microceratops
was about the
size of a rabbit.
Spot 15.

Saurornithoides
had large eyes
and may have
been able to
see in the dark.
Find ten.

Small mammals
ran through the
undergrowth,
catching insects
to eat. Spot five.

Bactrosaurus had
hundreds of teeth
for chewing
tough leaves.
Spot seven.

Velociraptor
means "speedy
killer". It was a
vicious meat-
eater. Spot six.

Gallimimus ran on
its back legs like
an ostrich, but it
didn't have any
feathers. Find 11.

Avimimus was unusual,
because it had feathers
on its body. Spot seven.

Homalocephale had a
thick skull with knobs
on the sides.
Spot three.

19

The last dinosaurs

During the late Cretaceous Period, there were more types of dinosaurs than at any other point in history. But then, about 64 million years ago, the dinosaurs suddenly died out.

Parasaurolophus used a tube on its head to make trumpet-like noises. Spot six.

Styracosaurus looked very fierce, but it only ate plants. Can you spot one?

Corythosaurus had a crest-like helmet on its head. Spot three.

Edmontosaurus lived in groups for protection against predators. Spot eight.

Panoplosaurus had spikes on its sides, but its belly was unprotected. Find two.

Pachycephalosaurus males had head-butting contests. Can you find five?

Triceratops weighed twice as much as an elephant. Spot four adults and two young.

Euoplocephalus may have swung the club on the end of its tail at attackers. Find three.

Ferocious hunter Tyrannosaurus was taller than a modern giraffe Spot one.

Stenonychosaurus may have been clever, because it had a big brain. Find seven.

Ichythornis was one of the first birds. Find six.

Struthiomimus looked like an ostrich, but with no feathers. Spot nine.

Stegoceras belonged to a group of dinosaurs called dome heads. Spot seven.

Pentaceratops had a neck frill which reached halfway down its back. Spot three.

Nodosaurus means "lumpy reptile". Spot two.

Dromaeosaurus killed larger dinosaurs by hunting in packs. Spot 12.

Woodland mammals

When the dinosaurs died out, mammals took their place. Mammals are warm-blooded animals. They have fur or hair, give birth to babies and feed them with milk.

Tetonis gripped onto branches with its strong hands and feet.
Spot five.

These bats hunted insects at night and slept during the day.
Spot five.

Hyrachus was about the size of a pig. It could run very fast.
Spot six.

Uintatherium was as large as a rhino, with six bony lumps on its head.
Spot one.

Smilodectes used its long tail for balance as it climbed trees.
Spot four.

Hyracotherium was an ancient relative of horses.
Spot 11.

Coryphodon means "curved tusks". It may have used them to defend itself.
Spot three.

Mesonyx had teeth like a dog, but hooves instead of paws. Find three.

Diatryma was a giant bird. It stood 2m (6½ft) tall. Spot two.

Notharctus looked a little like a monkey. Spot seven.

Leptictidium was an omnivore, which means it ate plants and animals. Spot eight.

Oxyaena was a cat-like hunter that crept up on its prey. Spot two.

Venomous snakes curled around branches to sleep. Spot three.

Moeritherium probably lived in and around water. Spot one.

Eomanis had no teeth. It used its long tongue to lick up ants. Spot two.

Archaeotherium used its strong sense of smell to sniff out tasty roots. Spot ten.

The Ice ages

During the Ice ages, the climate switched between very warm and extremely cold, with thick snow and ice. Here you can see some of the animals that lived in these different climates.

Columbian mammoths had tusks over 4m (13ft) long. Spot four.

Long-horned bison had poor eyesight. Can you find 12?

Woolly rhinos pushed away the snow with their horns to reach grass. Spot one.

Male cave lions were larger than lions today, but they didn't have manes. Spot one.

Like modern camels, Western camels stored water in their humps. Spot two.

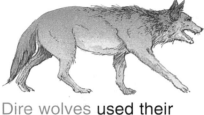

Dire wolves used their strong teeth to crush up bones. Find six.

Ground sloths had bony lumps under their skin for protection. Spot one.

24

Teratornis swooped down to feed on dead animals. Can you find two?

Cave bears went into caves to sleep through the coldest weather. Spot two.

Grey wolves lived and hunted in packs of up to ten animals. Find seven.

Arctic hares had white fur so wolves couldn't see them against the snow. Spot seven.

Herds of **ancient bison** roamed the plains in search of food. Spot nine.

Reindeer had wide feet to stop them from sinking into the snow. Find ten.

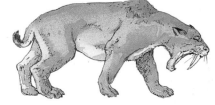

Sabre-toothed cats used their huge fangs to kill other animals. Spot two.

Woolly mammoths had thick, shaggy fur to keep them warm. Find four.

Western horses died out 10,000 years ago, but no one knows why. Find 12.

Death of the dinosaurs

About 64 million years ago, almost all the dinosaurs died out. No one is certain why. Most scientists believe that an enormous rock from space, measuring up to 10km (6 miles) across, may have hit the Earth.

Clouds of dust

When the rock hit the Earth, it would have caused a huge ball of fire to spread around the world. The rock would have smashed into tiny pieces, surrounding the planet with clouds of dust, rocks and water. The cloud would have blocked out the Sun's light, making the Earth cold and dark for months.

This picture shows what may have happened as the meteorite struck the Earth.

Huge clouds of dust spread out over the Earth, making it hard for creatures to breathe.

Creatures dying

This would have killed any creatures that needed warmth to survive. Without light, many plants must have died as well, leaving many of the dinosaurs with nothing to eat. The rock may also have caused massive earthquakes and huge tidal waves.

Creatures were killed or injured by pieces of flying rock.

Dinosaur puzzle

These dinosaurs are ones that you've seen already in the book. How much can you remember about them?

You may need to look back to help you with this puzzle. If you get really stuck, you'll find the answers on page 28.

1. Only one of these animals has an unusual covering of feathers on its body. Which one is it?

A   B   C   D   E

2. Can you guess which of these creatures was the first bird?

A   B   C   D   E

3. Which of these could kill another animal by stinging it?

A   B   C   D   E

4. Four of these are animals, and only one is a plant. Can you guess which one it is?

A   B   C   D   E

5. Which one of these dinosaurs did not eat meat?

A   B   C   D   E

6. Which of these fish could use its jointed fins to walk along the bottom of a lake?

A   B   C   D   E

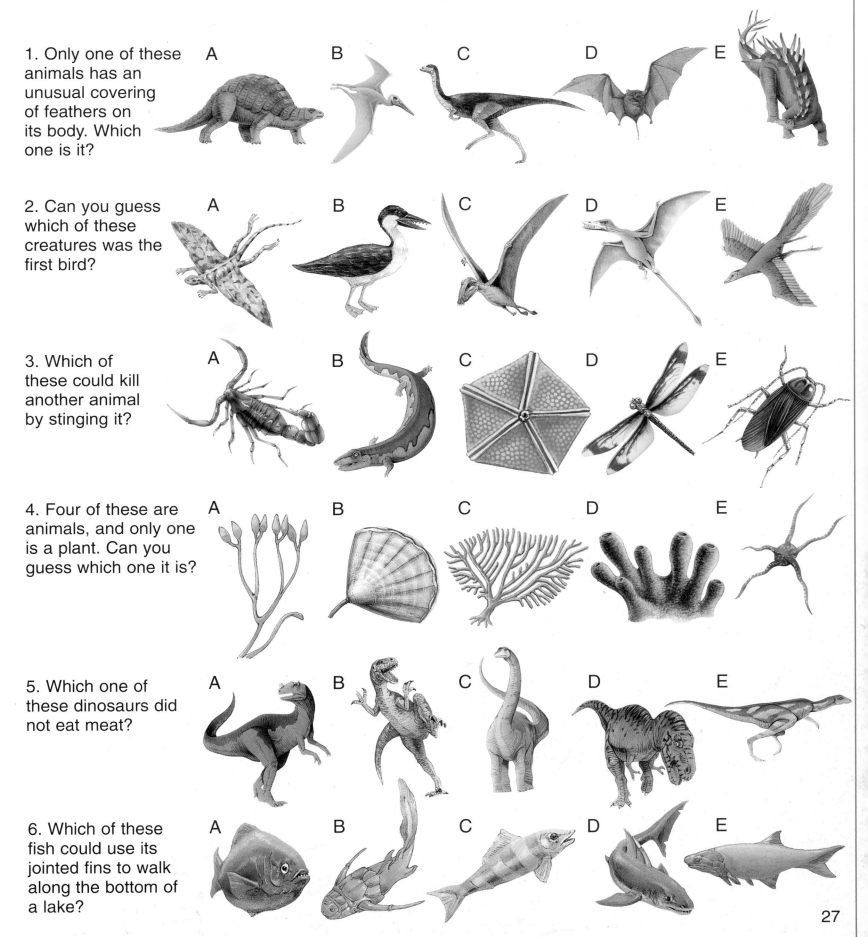

Answers

The keys on pages 28 to 31 show you where all the animals and plants you have been asked to spot appear on the pictures in this book. Use the keys if you get stuck trying to find a particular animal or plant.

The answers to the dinosaur puzzle on page 27 are as follows:
1. C
2. E
3. A
4. A
5. C
6. B

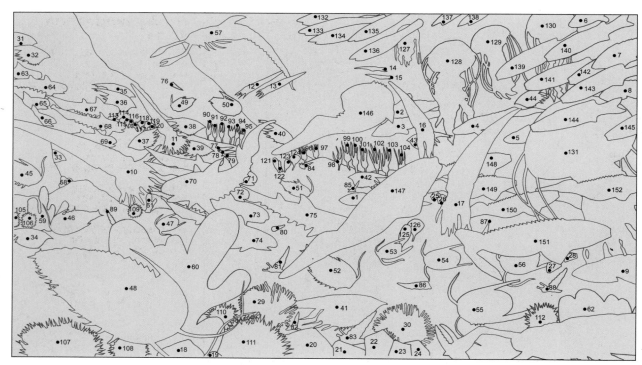

Shallow seas 4-5

Osteostracan fish, 1, 2, 3, 4, 5, 6, 7, 8, 9
Cephalopods, 10, 11, 12, 13, 14, 15, 16, 17
Starfish, 18, 19, 20, 21, 22, 23, 24, 25, 26, 27, 28
Graptolites, 29, 30
Shrimps, 31, 32, 33, 34, 35, 36, 37, 38, 39, 40, 41, 42, 43, 44
Trilobites, 45, 46, 47, 48, 49, 50, 51, 52, 53, 54, 55, 56
Eurypterid, 57
Sponges, 58, 59, 60, 61, 62
Nostolepis, 63, 64, 65, 66, 67, 68, 69, 70, 71, 72, 73, 74, 75
Marine snails, 76, 77, 78, 79, 80, 81, 82, 83, 84, 85, 86, 87, 88, 89
Sea-lillies, 90, 91, 92, 93, 94, 95, 96, 97, 98, 99, 100, 101, 102, 103, 104
Sea urchins, 105, 106, 107, 108, 109, 110, 111, 112
Brachiopods, 113, 114, 115, 116, 117, 118, 119, 120, 121, 122, 123, 124, 125, 126,
Jellyfish, 127, 128, 129, 130, 131
Heterostracan, 132, 133, 134, 135, 136, 137, 138
Thelodont, 139, 140, 141, 142, 143, 144, 145
Anapsid, 146, 147, 148, 149, 150, 151, 152

Living on the land 6-7

Ichthyostegopsis, 1,2
Panderichthys, 3, 4, 5
Horsetail plants, 6, 7, 8, 9, 10, 11, 12, 13, 14, 15, 16, 17, 18, 19, 20, 21
Water beetles, 22, 23, 24, 25, 26, 27, 28, 29, 30
Woodlice, 31, 32, 33, 34, 35, 36, 37, 38, 39, 40
Shrimps, 41, 42, 43, 44, 45, 46, 47, 48, 49, 50, 51, 52, 53, 54, 55
Eusthenopteron, 56, 57, 58
Mimia, 59, 60, 61, 62, 63, 64, 65, 66, 67, 68, 69, 70, 71, 72, 73, 74, 75, 76
Acanthostega, 77, 78, 79, 80, 81, 82, 83
Ctenacanthus, 84
Groenlandapis, 85, 86, 87, 88, 89
Ichthyostega, 90, 91, 92, 93
Ichthyostega's eggs, 94, 95, 96, 97
Aglaophyton, 98, 99, 100, 101, 102, 103
Clubmosses, 104, 105, 106, 107, 108, 109, 110, 111, 112
Bothriolepis, 113, 114, 115, 116, 117

Giant insects 8-9

Archaeothyris, 1, 2, 3
Land snails, 4, 5, 6, 7, 8, 9, 10, 11, 12, 13
Microsaurs, 14, 15, 16, 17, 18, 19, 20, 21, 22, 23, 24
Ophiderpeton, 25, 26, 27, 28, 29
Spiders, 30, 31, 32, 33, 34, 35, 36
Westlothiana, 37, 38, 39, 40, 41, 42, 43, 44, 45, 46
Gerrothorax, 47
Eogyrinus, 48, 49, 50, 51
Giant millipedes, 52, 53, 54, 55, 56
Giant Scorpion, 57, 58, 59
Gephyrostegus, 60, 61, 62, 63, 64, 65
Hylonomus, 66, 67, 68, 69, 70, 71, 72
Arthropleura, 73, 74, 75, 76, 77, 78
Cockroaches, 79, 80, 81, 82, 83, 84, 85, 86, 87, 88, 89, 90, 91, 92, 93
Meganeura, 94, 95, 96, 97
Pholidogaster, 98, 99

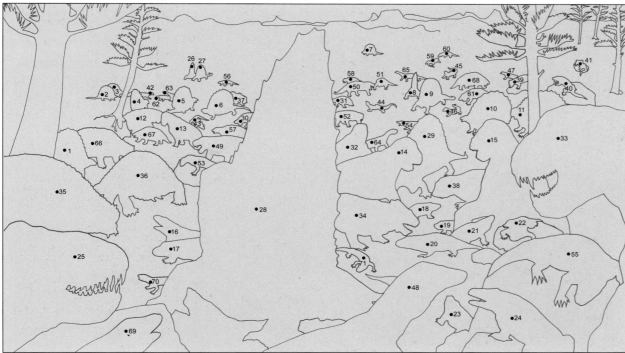
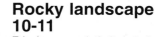

Rocky landscape 10-11

Edaphosaurus 1, 2, 3, 4, 5, 6, 7, 8, 9, 10, 11
Moschops, 12, 13, 14, 15,
Cacops, 16, 17, 18, 19, 20, 21, 22, 23, 24
Dimetrodon, 25, 26, 27, 28, 29
Eryops, 30, 31
Anteosaurus, 32, 33
Bradysaurus, 34
Scutosaurus, 35, 36, 37
Casea, 38, 39, 40, 41
Diadectes, 42, 43, 44, 45, 46, 47, 48
Sauroctonus, 49, 50, 51, 52
Seymouria, 53, 54, 55
Sphenacodon, 56, 57, 58, 59, 60, 61
Protorosaurus, 62, 63, 64, 65
Pareiasaurus, 66, 67, 68
Yougina, 69, 70, 71

The first dinosaurs 12-13

Saltopus, 1, 2, 3, 4, 5, 6, 7, 8, 9, 10
Syntarsus, 11, 12, 13, 14
Peteinosaurus, 15, 16, 17
Placerias, 18, 19, 20, 21, 22, 23, 24, 25, 26, 27
Desmatosuchus, 28, 29, 30
Coelophysis, 31, 32, 33, 34, 35, 36, 37
Thrinaxodon, 38, 39, 40, 41, 42
Stagonolepis, 43, 44, 45, 46
Anchisaurus, 47, 48, 49, 50, 51
Ticinosuchus, 52, 53, 54, 55, 56
Rutiodon, 57, 58
Plateosaurus, 59, 60, 61, 62, 63, 64
Staurikosaurus, 65, 66, 67, 68, 69, 70, 71
Terrestrisuchus, 72, 73, 74, 75, 76, 77, 78, 79
Cynognathus, 80
Kuehneosaurus, 81, 82, 83, 84

29

In the forest 14-15

Diplodocus, 1, 2, 3, 4, 5, 6
Dryosaurus, 7, 8, 9, 10, 11, 12, 13, 14, 15, 16, 17, 18, 19, 20, 21, 22, 23
Archaeopteryx, 24, 25, 26
Kentrosaurus, 27
Scaphognathus, 28, 29
Allosaurus, 30, 31, 32
Stegosaurus, 33, 34
Coelurus, 35, 36
Ornitholestes, 37, 38, 39
Camarasaurus, 40, 41, 42
Compsognathus, 43, 44, 45, 46, 47, 48, 49, 50
Ceratosaurus, 51
Camptosaurus, 52, 53
Apatosaurus, 54, 55, 56, 57, 58
Pteradactylus, 59, 60, 61, 62, 63, 64, 65, 66, 67, 68
Brachiosaurus, 69

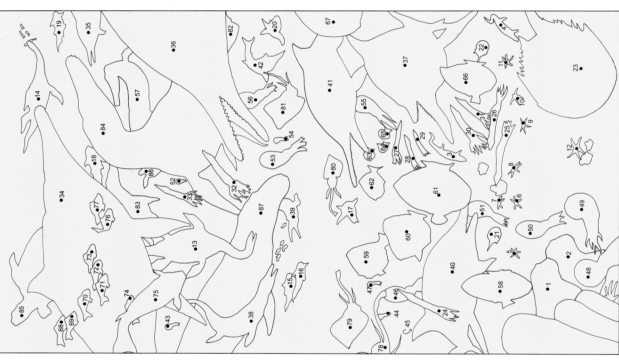

In the ocean 16-17

Pleurosaurus, 1, 2, 3, 4
Brittle stars, 5, 6, 7, 8, 9, 10, 11, 12
Plesiosaurus, 13, 14
Sharks, 15, 16, 17, 18, 19, 20
King crabs, 21, 22, 23
Belemnites, 24, 25, 26, 27, 28, 29, 30, 31, 32, 33
Ichythyosaurus, 34, 35, 36, 37
Geosaurus, 38, 39
Eurhinosaurus, 40, 41, 42
Ammonites, 43, 44, 45, 46, 47, 48, 49, 50, 51, 52, 53, 54, 55, 56
Teleosaurus, 57
Fish, 58, 59, 60, 61, 62, 63, 64, 65, 66, 67, 68, 69, 70, 71, 72, 73, 74, 75, 76, 77
Banjo fish, 78, 79, 80, 81, 82
Rhomaleosaurus, 83, 84
Pleurosternon, 85, 86
Liopleurodon, 87

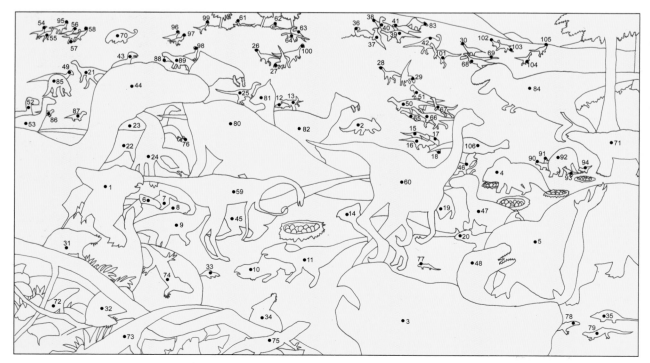

Dusty desert 18-19

Protoceratops, 1, 2, 3, 4, 5
Microsceratops, 6, 7, 8, 9, 10, 11, 12, 13, 14, 15, 16, 17, 18, 19 ,20
Saurornithoides, 21, 22, 23, 24, 25, 26, 27, 28, 29, 30
Mammals, 31, 32, 33, 34, 35
Bractrosaurus, 36, 37, 38, 39, 40, 41, 42
Velociraptor, 43, 44, 45, 46, 47, 48
Homalocephale, 49, 50, 51
Avimimus, 52, 53, 54, 55, 56, 57, 58
Gallimimus, 59, 60, 61, 62, 63, 64, 65, 66, 67, 68, 69
Pinacosaurus, 70, 71
Lizards, 72, 73, 74, 75, 76, 77, 78, 79
Saurolophus, 80, 81, 82, 83,
Tarbosaurus, 84
Psittacosaurus, 85, 86, 87, 88, 89, 90, 91, 92, 93, 94
Oviraptor, 95, 96, 97, 98, 99, 100, 101, 102, 103, 104, 105, 106

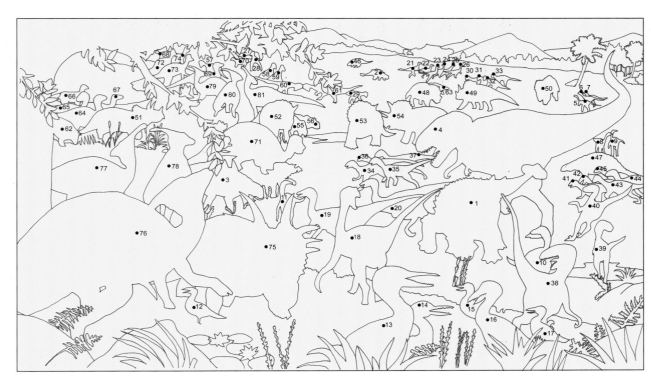

The last dinosaurs 20-21

Euoplocephalus, 1, 2, 3
Tyrannosaurus, 4
Stenonychosaurus, 5, 6, 7, 8, 9, 10, 11
Ichythornis, 12, 13, 14, 15, 16, 17
Struthiomimus, 18, 19, 20, 21, 22, 23, 24, 25, 26
Stegoceras, 27, 28, 29, 30, 31, 32, 33
Dromaeosaurus, 34, 35, 36, 37, 38, 39, 40, 41, 42, 43, 44, 45
Nodosaurus, 46, 47
Pentaceratops, 48, 49, 50
Triceratops, 51, 52, 53, 54, 55, 56
Pachycephalosaurus, 57, 58, 59, 60, 61
Panoplosaurus, 62, 63
Edmontosaurus, 64, 65, 66, 67, 68, 69, 70, 71
Corythosaurus, 72, 73, 74
Stryracosaurus, 75
Parasaurolophus, 76, 77, 78, 79, 80, 81

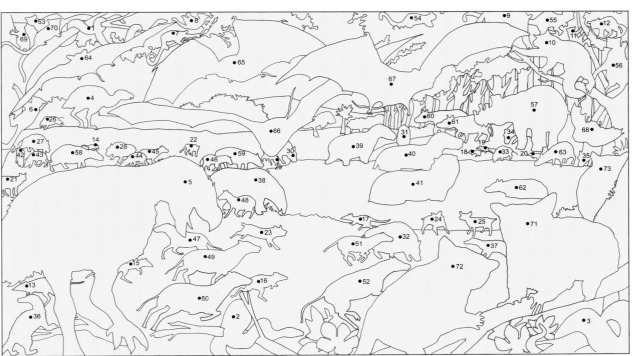

Woodland mammals 22-23

Snake, 1, 2, 3
Diatryma, 4, 5
Notharctus, 6, 7, 8, 9, 10, 11, 12
Leptictidium, 13, 14, 15, 16, 17, 18, 19, 20
Oxyaena, 21, 22
Mexonyx, 23, 24, 25
Archaeotherium, 26, 27, 28, 29, 30, 31, 32, 33, 34, 35
Eomanis, 36, 37
Moeritherium, 38
Coryphodon, 39, 40, 41
Hyracotherium, 42, 43, 44, 45, 46, 47, 48, 49, 50, 51, 52
Smilodectes, 53, 54, 55, 56
Uintatherium, 57
Hyrachus, 58, 59, 60, 61, 62, 63
Bats, 64, 65, 66, 67, 68
Tetonis, 69, 70, 71, 72, 73

The Ice ages 24-25

Teratornis, 1, 2
Cave bears, 3, 4
Grey Wolves, 5, 6, 7, 8, 9, 10, 11
Arctic hares, 12, 13, 14, 15, 16, 17, 18
Ancient bison, 19, 20, 21, 22, 23, 24, 25, 26, 27
Reindeer, 28, 29, 30, 31, 32, 33, 34, 35, 36, 37
Western horses, 38, 39, 40, 41, 42, 43, 44, 45, 46, 47, 48, 49
Woolly mammoths, 50, 51, 52, 53
Sabre-toothed cats, 54, 55
Ground sloth, 56
Dire wolves, 57, 58, 59, 60, 61, 62
Camels, 63, 64
Cave lion, 65
Woolly rhino, 66
Long-horned bison, 67, 68, 69, 70, 71, 72, 73, 74, 75, 76, 77, 78
Columbian mammoths, 79, 80, 81, 82

Index

First published in 2000 by Usborne Publishing Ltd.,
Usborne House, 83-85 Saffron Hill, London, EC1N 8RT,
England. www.usborne.com

Copyright © 2000 Usborne Publishing Ltd.
The name Usborne and the devices ♀ ⊕ are Trade Marks
of Usborne Publishing Ltd.

First Published in America 2001
Printed in Spain